PLEASE READ THIS

I'm warning you. If you turn the page, you are going to see some terrible things. Some really terrible things. This book is full of them.

Didn't you read the title?

Just about everything in this book is terrible.

You're probably going to turn the page, anyway, aren't you?

Okay.

Go ahead.

YOU'VE BEEN WARNED.

Twelve
Terr

idle Things

Marty Kelley

TRICYCLE PRESS
BERKELEY | TORONTO

1 Oooopsie!

2 There's nothing under the bed...

There's nothing under the bed...

There's
nothing
under
the bed...

3 Say AHHH...

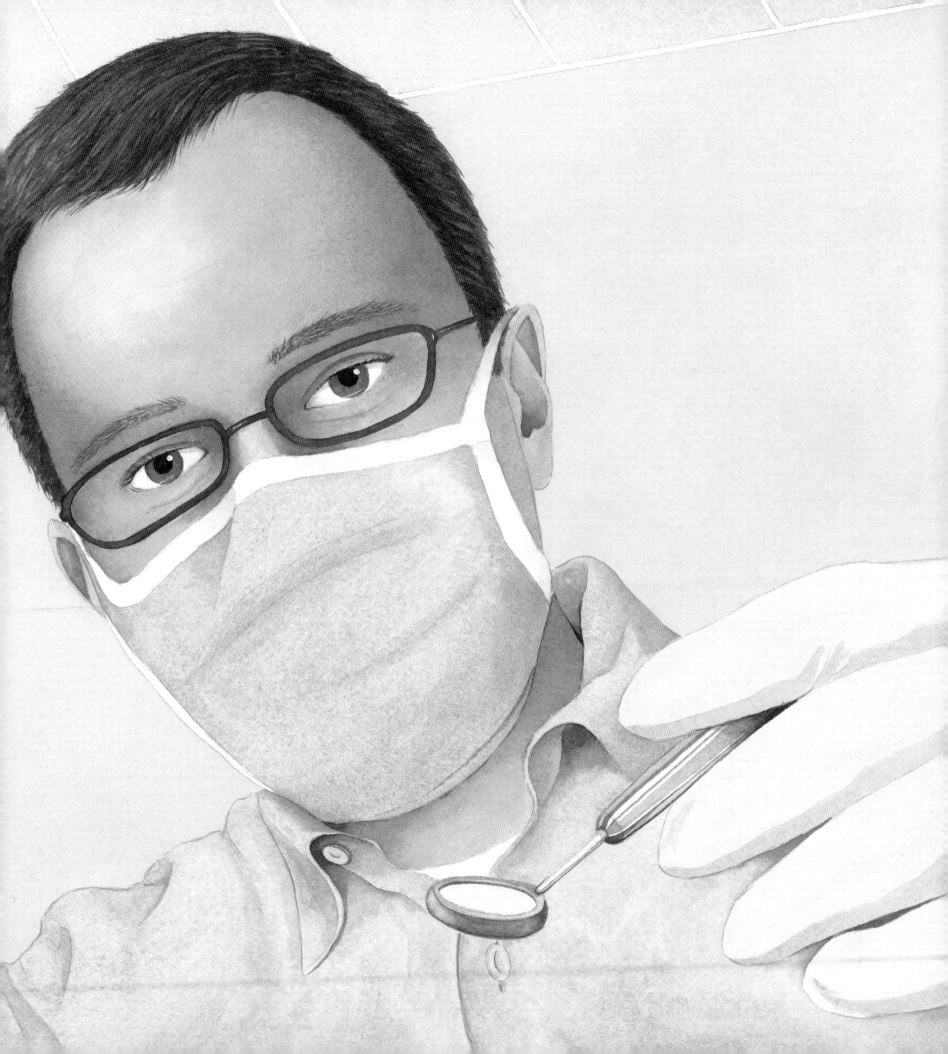

4 HOLD STILL.
I'm almost done.

5 *Oh my goodness,* just look at those **CHEEKS.**

6 I've got one last surprise for the birthday kid!

7 This must be our NEW student.

8 No, we are NOT there yet!

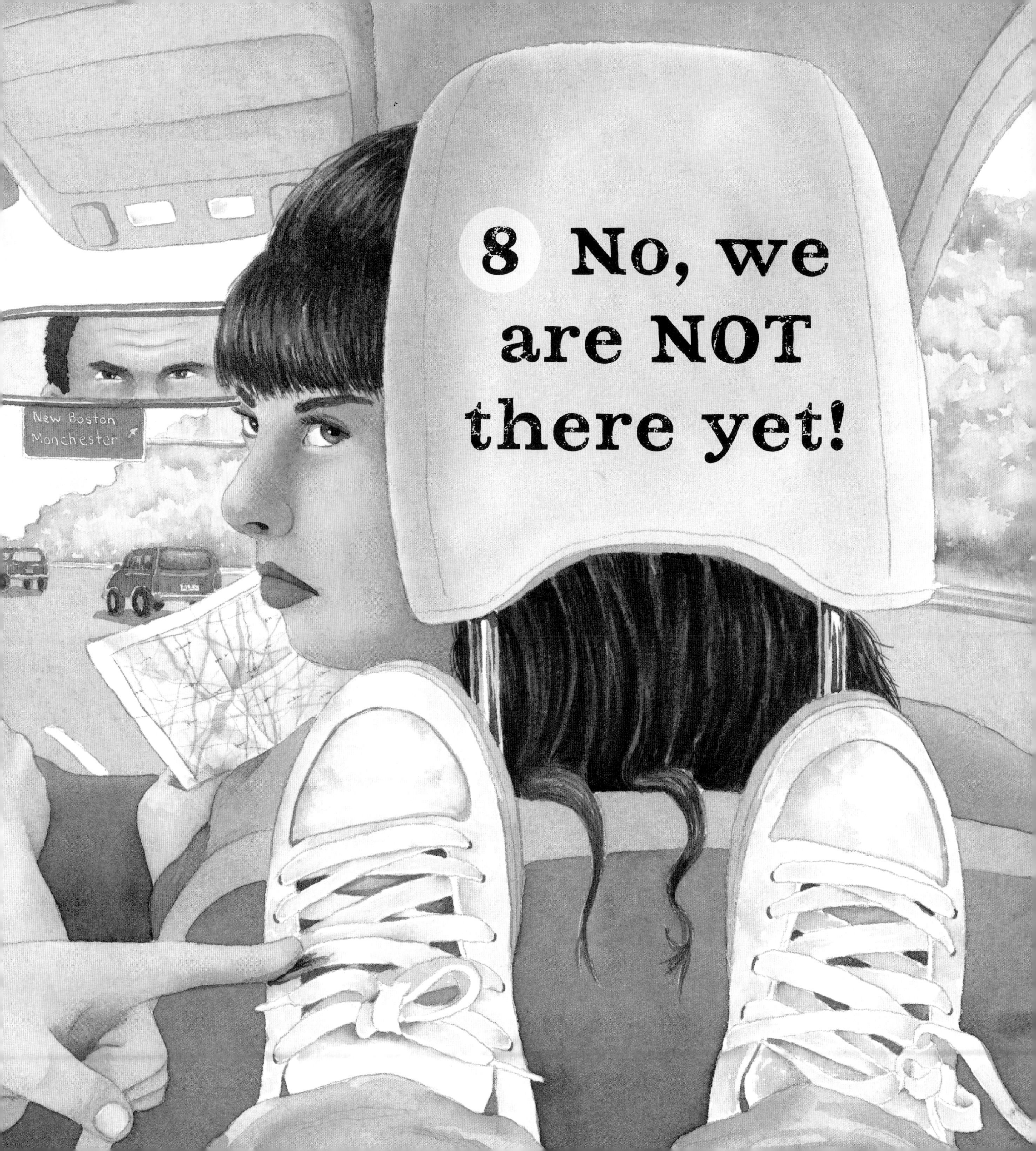

9 Goodbye, **Goldie.**

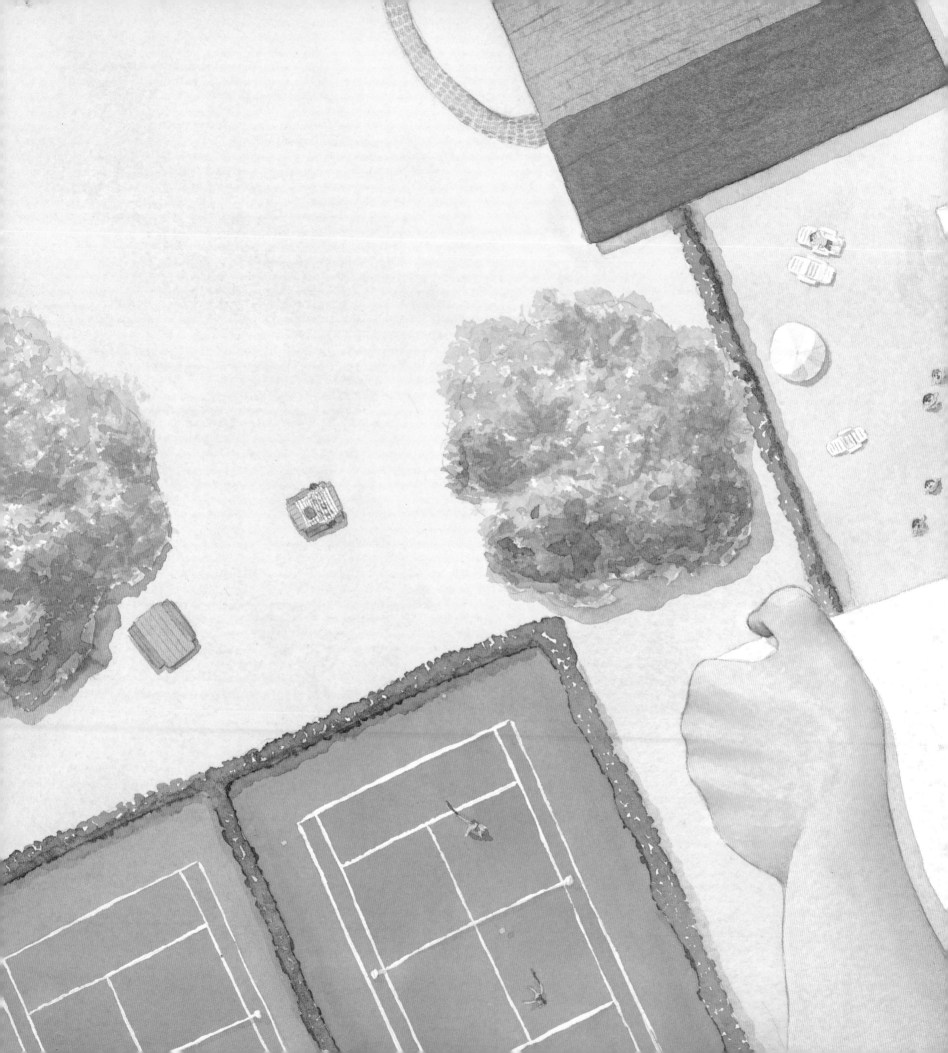

10 Come on already...
JUMP!

11 What do you mean you don't like gravy?

12 Smell THIS, doofus.